Actions
Las Acciones

by Mary Berendes • illustrated by Kathleen Petelinsek

Published in the United States of America by The Child's World®
1980 Lookout Drive • Mankato, MN 56003-1705
800-599-READ • www.childsworld.com

Acknowledgments
The Child's World®: Mary Berendes, Publishing Director
The Design Lab: Kathleen Petelinsek, Design and Page Production

Language Adviser: Ariel Strichartz

Library of Congress Cataloging-in-Publication Data
Berendes, Mary.
 Actions = Las acciones / by Mary Berendes ; illustrated by Kathleen Petelinsek.
    p. cm. — (Wordbooks = Libros de palabras)
  ISBN 978-1-59296-987-6 (library bound : alk. paper)
 1. Spanish language—Verbs. 2. Spanish language—Textbooks for foreign
speakers—English. I. Petelinsek, Kathleen. II. Title. III. Title: Acciones. IV. Series.
  PC4271.B47 2008
  468.2'421—dc22   2007046562

skip
brincar

march
marchar

flutter
revolotear

jump
saltar

wave
saludar con
la mano

walk
caminar

jog
hacer footing

3

climb
trepar

fly
volar

run
correr

slide
deslizar

flutter
revolotear

4

shine
brillar

smile
sonreír

swing
columpiarse

5

1 2 3 4 5 6 7 8 9 10

count
contar

Spelling
Words
1. cat
2. boy
3. dog

write
escribir

teach
enseñar

stand
estar de pie

6

study
estudiar

read
leer

learn
aprender

sit
sentarse

catch
coger

flutter
revolotear

paddle
chapotear

8

snorkel
bucear con
esnórkel

splash
salpicar

swim
nadar

float
flotar

9

stir
remover

wash
lavar

flip
voltear

boil
hervir

fry
freír

cook
cocinar

bake
hornear

11

George's Diner

lick
lamer

slurp
sorber
ruidosamente

13

Talent

perform
actuar

bow
hacer una
reverencia

dance
bailar

act
representar

clap
aplaudir

Show

sing
cantar

tumble
dar volteretas

SCORE

Home	Visitors
2	1

collide
chocar

run
correr

watch
mirar

fall
caerse

kick
dar patadas

shout
gritar

fly
volar

leap
saltar

hide
esconderse

dig
escarbar

swim
nadar

18

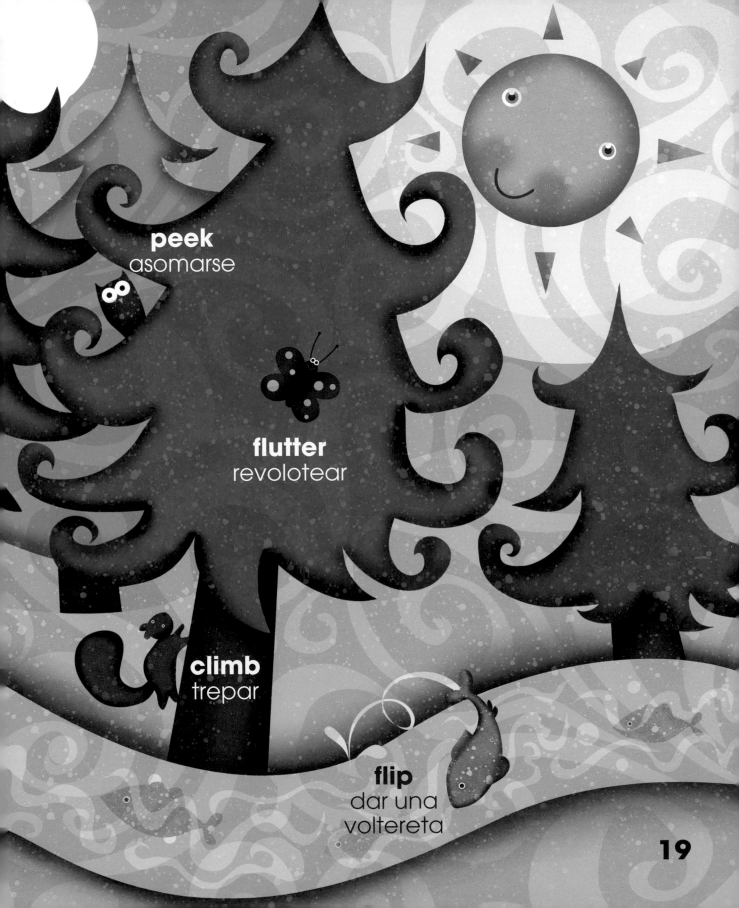

peek
asomarse

flutter
revolotear

climb
trepar

flip
dar una
voltereta

19

pick
cortar

dig
cavar

plant
plantar

20

shine
brillar

grow
crecer

pollinate
polinizar

water
regar

21

comb
peinarse

brush (teeth)
cepillarse los dientes

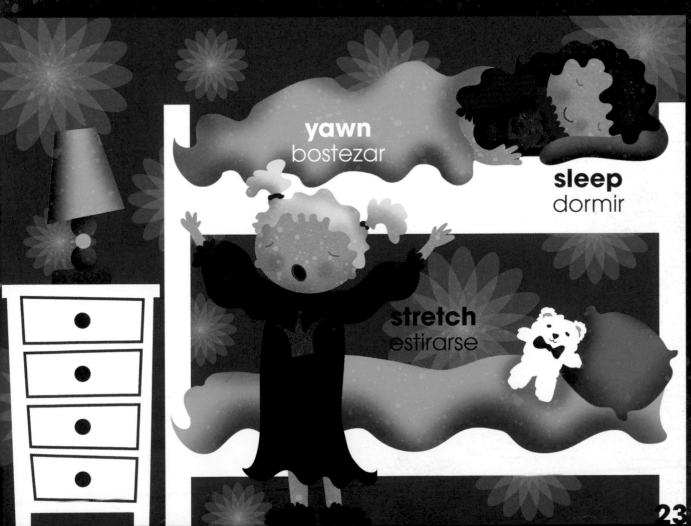

yawn
bostezar

sleep
dormir

stretch
estirarse

23

word list
lista de palabras

to act	representar	**to march**	marchar
actions	las acciones	**to paddle**	chapotear
to bake	hornear	**to peek (out)**	asomarse
to bite	morder	**to perform**	actuar
to boil	hervir	**to pick (flowers)**	cortar
to bow	hacer una reverencia	**to plant**	plantar
to brush (teeth)	cepillarse los dientes	**to pollinate**	polinizar
to catch	coger	**to read**	leer
to chew	masticar	**to run**	correr
to clap	aplaudir	**to shine**	brillar
to climb	trepar	**to shout**	gritar
to collide	chocar	**to sing**	cantar
to comb (hair)	peinarse	**to sit (down)**	sentarse
to cook	cocinar	**to skip**	brincar
to count	contar	**to sleep**	dormir
to dance	bailar	**to slide**	deslizar
to dig (a tunnel)	escarbar	**to slurp**	sorber ruidosamente
to dig (with a shovel)	cavar	**to smile**	sonreír
to drink	beber	**to snorkel**	bucear con esnórkel
to eat	comer	**to splash**	salpicar
to fall (down)	caerse	**to stand**	estar de pie
to (do a) flip	dar una voltereta	**to stir**	remover
to flip (something)	voltear	**to stretch**	estirarse
to float	flotar	**to study**	estudiar
to flutter	revolotear	**to swim**	nadar
to fly	volar	**to swing**	columpiarse
to fry	freír	**to teach**	enseñar
to grow	crecer	**to tumble**	dar volteretas
to hide	esconderse	**to walk**	caminar
to jog	hacer footing	**to wash (dishes)**	lavar
to jump	saltar	**to watch**	mirar
to kick	dar patadas	**to water (plants)**	regar
to leap	saltar	**to wave**	saludar con la mano
to learn	aprender	**to write**	escribir
to lick (foods)	lamer	**to yawn**	bostezar